IS THERE ROOM ON THE BUS?

A round-the-world counting story

HELEN PIERS

Illustrated by

HANNAH GIFFARD

FRANCES LINCOLN

Sam had a bus.

It was a bit battered, rickety and rusty.
But one day Sam got to work on his bus.
He painted it and polished it and did
some repairs.

Then he set off to drive around the world.

Sam had not gone far when he met a lion.

"I'm all alone," the lion said. "Can I come with you?"

"Of course," Sam said. "I enjoy company."

So Sam
  and **one** lonely lion
    set off around the world.

They'd not gone far when they met two cows.

"Can we come too?" the cows mooed. "We're in a bad moo-ood. A drive around the world would cheer us up."

"Plenty of room," Sam said.

So Sam,
one lonely lion
and two cross cows
set off around the world.

They'd not gone far when they met three walruses.
"We're wet," said the walruses, "but we'll soon dry off."

So Sam,
    one lonely lion,
       two cross cows
         and **three** wet walruses
           set off around the world.

          Plenty of room on the bus.

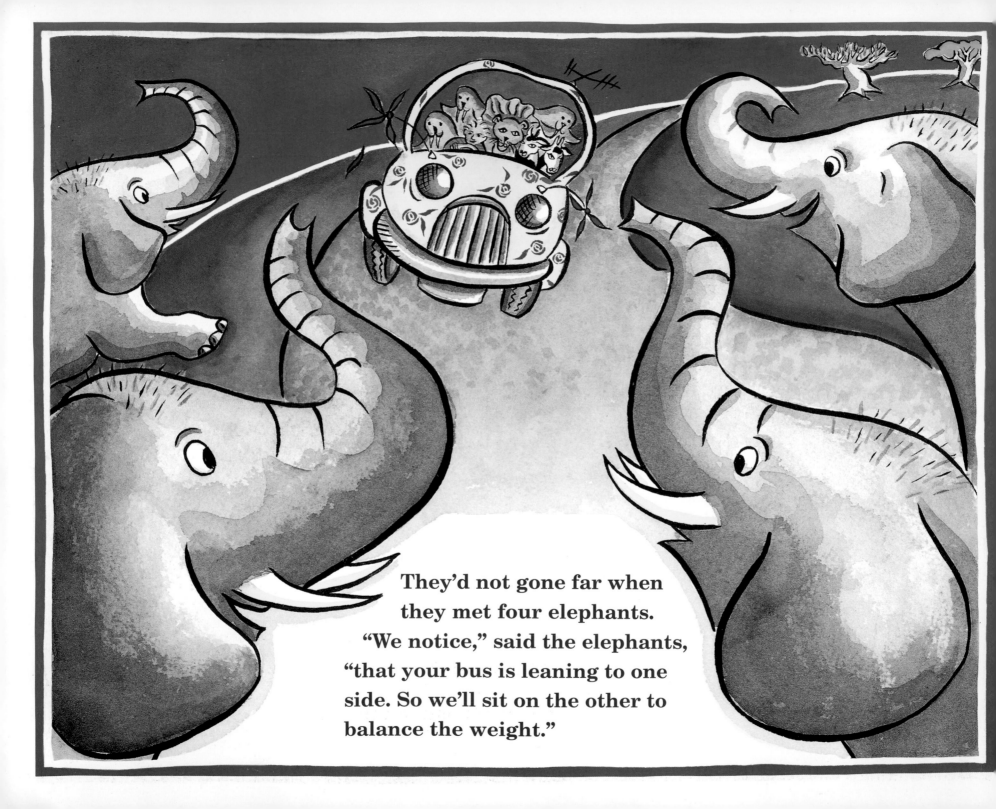

They'd not gone far when
they met four elephants.
"We notice," said the elephants,
"that your bus is leaning to one
side. So we'll sit on the other to
balance the weight."

So Sam,
   one lonely lion,
      two cross cows,
         three wet walruses
            and **four** energetic elephants
         set off around the world.

         Plenty of room on the bus.

They'd not gone far when they met five frogs.
"We've got the fidgets," the frogs said. "A drive
around the world will quieten us down."

So Sam,
    one lonely lion,
      two cross cows,
        three wet walruses,
          four energetic elephants
           and **five** fidgety frogs
             set off around the world.

              Plenty of room on the bus.

They'd not gone far when they met six pigs.
   "We'll dance and sing you a song as we go along,"
the pigs squealed.

So Sam,
  one lonely lion,
    two cross cows,
      three wet walruses,
        four energetic elephants,
          five fidgety frogs
            and **six** prancing pigs
              set off around the world.

              Plenty of room on the bus.

They'd not gone far when they met seven sheep.
  "Do you mind if we come too?" the sheep timidly asked.
"We'll squeeze in the back, out of the way."
  "Oh sorry, so v-e-e-e-ry sorry!" they bleated, as they
trod on everyone's toes.

So Sam, **one** lonely lion, **two** cross cows, **three** wet walruses,
four energetic elephants, **five** fidgety frogs, **six** prancing pigs
and **seven** shy sheep set off around the world.

Is there still room on the bus?   Y-e-s, j-u-s-t a-b-o-u-t . . .

They'd not gone far when they
met eight tigers.
"Can we come too? We've been
walking for miles," said the tigers.

So Sam,
   one lonely lion,
      two cross cows,
         three wet walruses,
            four energetic elephants,
               five fidgety frogs,
                  six prancing pigs,
                     seven shy sheep
                        and **eight** tired tigers with sore feet
                        set off around the world.

Is there still room on the bus?
Yes, but it's a bit of a squash...

They had not gone far when they met nine crocodiles.
"Move along there, please," grumbled the crocodiles.
"Other people want to get on the bus too, you know."

So Sam,
one lonely lion,
two cross cows,
three wet walruses,
four energetic elephants,
five fidgety frogs,
six prancing pigs,
seven shy sheep,
eight tired tigers
and nine crotchety crocodiles
set off around the world.

But then... they met ten bumble-bees.

"Buzz! Wait for uz!
Uz is coming!" buzzed
the bumble-bees.
"NO! NO! NO! There's
no room for bothersome
bees on this bus."
"But look! Little uz
doezn't need any room!
Buzz-z-z-z!"

Oh dear! What a to-do,
what a hullabaloo–
one lonely lion,
  two cross cows,
    three wet walruses,
four energetic elephants,
  five fidgety frogs,
    six prancing pigs,
seven shy sheep,
  eight tigers with sore feet
  and **nine** crotchety crocodiles
    all pushed
      and shoved
        and...

...burst out of the bus to escape
from those bothersome bees!

"Never mind," Sam said. "A coat of paint, a few repairs, and then I'll set off again – right round the world this time."

And...

"We'll come too," said **1** lonely lion   **2** cross cows

3 wet walruses

4 energetic elephants

5 fidgety frogs

6 prancing pigs

7 shy sheep

8 tired tigers

and 9 crotchety crocodiles...

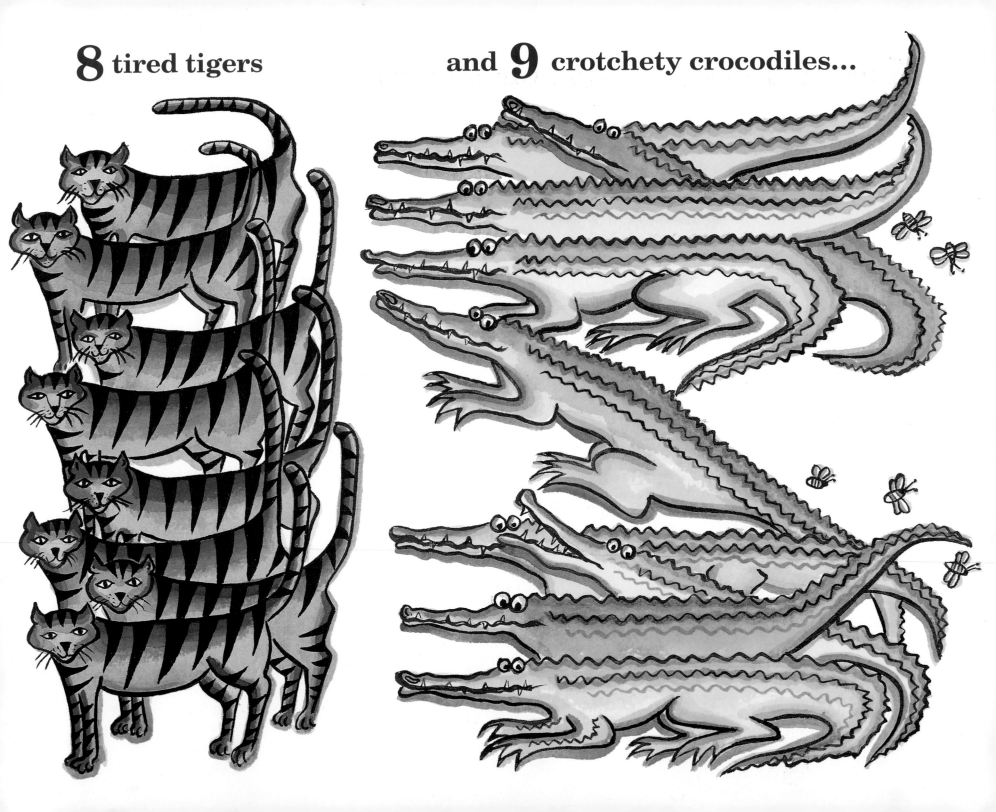

Luckily, the **10** bothersome bees flew away.

To Maia and Olivia – H.P.
To our new arrival Caspar, with love – H.G.

First published in Great Britain in 1996 by
Frances Lincoln Limited, 4 Torriano Mews
Torriano Avenue, London NW5 2RZ

British Library Cataloguing in Publication Data
available on request

ISBN 0-7112-0947-2 hardback
ISBN 0-7112-0951-0 paperback

Set in New Century Schoolbook Bold

Printed in Hong Kong

3 5 7 9 8 6 4

MORE PICTURE BOOKS IN PAPERBACK FROM FRANCES LINCOLN

RED FOX
Hannah Giffard

A bold, brilliantly coloured picture book for younger children in which Red Fox
has to brave the town to find food for his new family.

Suitable for National Curriculum English – Reading, Key Stage 1
Scottish Guidelines English Language – Reading, Levels A and B; Environmental Studies – Levels A and B

ISBN 0-7112-0747-X

DOWN BY THE POND
Margrit Cruickshank
Illustrated by Dave Saunders

Fox thinks he can slink through the farmyard without being noticed. But the cow, the pig
and all the other animals catch a glimpse of him, and in a glorious hullabaloo, they soon show
who's in charge. A medley of animal noises and a twist in the tale make this rhyming story,
with its amusing illustrations and die-cut pages, a delight for all young readers.

Suitable for National Curriculum English – Reading, Key Stage 1
Scottish Guidelines English Language – Reading, Levels A and B

ISBN 0-7112-0978-2

FIDDLE-I-FEE
Jakki Wood

An exuberant retelling of a well-known nursery rhyme that will have children singing
along in no time. Margaret Lion has arranged the accompanying melody, based on
a traditional folk song, for piano and guitar.

Suitable for National Curriculum English – Reading, Key Stage 1
Scottish Guidelines English Language – Reading, Level A

ISBN 0-7112-0860-3

Frances Lincoln titles are available from all good bookshops

Helen Piers studied at the Royal Academy of Dramatic Art
and the Central School of Art. She is the author and photographer
of a number of animal story books for Methuen, and has also
created the highly successful Looking After Your Pet series
for Frances Lincoln. Helen Piers lives in London.

Hannah Giffard was born in London and studied at
the Norwich School of Art and Bristol Polytechnic. Her parents
are both artists, so she was surrounded by art from an early age.
Her first two books for Frances Lincoln, *Red Fox* and *Red Fox on
the Move*, were enthusiastically reviewed and both were selected
as Children's Books of the Year. She has since created
the Early Days Board Books for Frances Lincoln.